E   Kulling,Monica
Kul

Queen in disguise

JEDI READERS

STAR WARS®

EPISODE I

QUEEN in DISGUISE

A Step 2 Book

BY MONICA KULLING
ILLUSTRATED BY JOHN ALVIN

Random House
New York

LUCAS BOOKS

Queen Amidala was
the new Queen of Naboo.
She lived in a grand palace.
She wore beautiful gowns.

Five handmaidens
helped her to dress.
They helped fix her hair.
Their names were Yané, Sabé,
Rabé, Eirtaé, and Saché.

Captain Panaka led
the Queen's security force.
"I have a plan
to keep you safe from danger,"
said Captain Panaka.

Queen Amidala looked out
her throne-room window.
"But Naboo is peaceful,"
she said.
"It is still wise to have a plan,"
said Captain Panaka.

He showed Queen Amidala
a secret room.
"If you are ever in danger,
you must come here,"
said Captain Panaka.
"You will dress as a handmaiden.
And one of your handmaidens
will dress as you."
This plan worried Queen Amidala.
"I do not want a handmaiden
to put herself in danger
for my sake," she said.

"Your handmaidens
   are trained to protect you,"
   said Captain Panaka.
"Let me show you," he said.
   Queen Amidala agreed
   to visit the training area.
   But she wanted to do more.
   She looked at the handmaidens'
   training outfits.

The Queen had an idea.

"I want to be trained too,"

she said.

Captain Panaka left the palace.

A handmaiden followed him.

Her name was Padmé.

But she was really

the Queen in disguise!

Her handmaidens must not

find out who she was.

She did not want them to worry.

Captain Panaka and Padmé
came to a forest.
"This is where
the training area is,"
said Captain Panaka.

"Watch your handmaidens,"
said Captain Panaka.
"They are quick and strong."

A security officer watched

the handmaidens

practice a drill.

They took turns

running through a course.

As they ran,

training droids fired

stun blasts at them.

It was Yané's turn.

She ran up a hill.

A training droid fired at her.

Yané did a quick back flip.

The droid's shot missed.

Yané fired back with
her training laser.
The beam
hit the droid's target zone.
The droid was stopped
in its tracks.

Padmé turned to Sabé.

"That was a good shot,"
said Padmé.

"Yes," said Sabé.

"We will fight
to protect our Queen."

Padmé smiled.

Her secret was safe!

Sabé did not know

Padmé *was* the Queen.

Eirtaé was up next.

She ran from rock to rock.

She jumped over the wall.

She rolled out of the way

of stun blasts.

Eirtaé aimed her laser.

Zing! Zing! Zing!

She stopped three droids.

"Good aim," said Captain Panaka.

Now it was Rabé's turn.

She ran for the wall.

A droid fired.

The stun blast hit Rabé

in the arm.

Yow!

The stun blast really stung!

Rabé ran behind a tree.

She fired at the droid.

Zing!

She hit the droid's target zone,

but it did not shut down.

Padmé and Sabé tried too.

But even two laser shots

at the same time

did not stop the droid.

Rabé knew she had
to get away from that droid.
It was programmed to target her.
And the stinging blasts
were too much to take!
Rabé ran for the waterfall.
It would be a good place
to hide.

Captain Panaka

was too far away to help.

"We have to stop that droid," said Padmé.

"But first we have to catch it,"
said Sabé.

Padmé and Sabé
raced after the droid.

Rabé climbed up the rocks

beside the waterfall.

The droid was right behind her!

The rocks were jagged

and slippery.

But Rabé was a good climber.

Another stun blast
hit Rabé in the leg.
She had to reach
the ledge quickly,
or she would fall!

The other handmaidens
ran up to the waterfall.
"What can we do?" asked Yané.
"Go tell Droid Control
to shut down the droid,"
Sabé told her.
"We don't have much time,"
said Padmé.
"Sabé and I will try
to knock out that droid.
But we will have to get closer."

Padmé and Sabé climbed
up the hill beside the waterfall.
"There she is," said Sabé.
She pointed at Rabé
on the ledge.

Rabé was safe behind the water.

But the droid was still

after her!

Padmé had an idea.

"Fire your cable shooter
at that tree up there,"
she said to Sabé.

Sabé fired.

Zip!

The cable hit the tree
and held fast.

Padmé grabbed
on to the cable.
She swung out over the falls!
She was headed
right for the droid.

With one swift kick,

she knocked the droid

into the falls.

It was swept away and

smashed onto the rocks below.

Padmé swung back and
leaped onto the ledge
where Rabé was hiding.
Rabé was happy to see her.
They were both safe!

But Rabé had twisted her ankle.

"I will help you," said Padmé.

Padmé held on to the cable.

Rabé put her arm

around Padmé.

"Hang on tight," said Padmé.

They swung from

rock to rock.

Water rushed past them.

Finally, Padmé and Rabé
reached the ground.
They were safe and sound!
Captain Panaka was there.

"We did it," Padmé said to Sabé.

She was very proud.

So was Captain Panaka.

"You saved Rabé's life,"
Captain Panaka said to Padmé.
"You are a brave Queen."
The handmaidens were shocked.

Padmé was really
Queen Amidala!
"I'm glad to see
that my handmaidens
are so well trained,"
she said.

What a wonderful surprise!
The handmaidens
were proud to know that
their Queen was so brave.
Now they also knew
she was a loyal friend.

www.randomhouse.com/kids
www.starwars.com

Library of Congress Cataloging-in-Publication Data
Kulling, Monica.
Star Wars, Episode I. Queen in disguise / by Monica Kulling ; illustrated by John Alvin.
p. cm. — (Step into reading) (Jedi readers. A step 2 book)
SUMMARY: While training in secret on Naboo, Queen Amidala comes to the aid of one of her handmaidens.
ISBN 0-375-80429-3 (trade) — ISBN 0-375-90429-8 (lib. bdg.)
[1. Science Fiction.] I. Title: Queen in disguise. II. Alvin, John, ill. III. Title.
IV. Series. V. Jedi readers. Step 2 book.
PZ7.K9490155 Sar 2000 [E]—dc21 99-041657

Printed in the United States of America March 2000 10 9 8 7 6 5 4 3 2 1